WAKE THE DEAD

JACK KELLY

DEDICATION

Restoration
Reconstruction
Rebuild

New Orleans
Proud to call it Home

ACKNOWLEDGMENTS

Thanks for the Internet and Google Search
for all the assists large and small.
Thanks goes to ADW whose ears I've bent,
and who read the story a time or two
with helpful comments and suggestions.

AUTHOR'S NOTES

The City of New Orleans is once again both the setting and a character in this story. And, once again, no effort to accuracy was attempted in measuring distance, or direction, or time for that matter to move between any two points. With a small possibility of less attention to it than before.
Any faults are strictly the authors and probably intentional.

Anniversary

It's August and the anniversary looms. Hanging over the city like a shadow, like a shade lingering in this most haunted city like a twist of irony. Shimmering like a mirage in the heat. The date approaches but remains unspoken of, still far enough away to be ignored and tucked into the back of the city's collective consciousness, but also too close for it to be completely ignored. Another hurricane season hovers off in the Gulf like it has every year, for the hundreds of years the city has perched here in the bend of a crooked river. An ever threatening menace projected over a city still raw from the last encounters.

There'd been talk of not saving the city after the previous catastrophe. A debate of the worth versus the cost of doing so. Judgments by people viewing from a distance with a skewed view of a city with *ahem*, a colorful reputation bordering on notorious, or is it the other way round?

There but for the grace of god as a thought and a wish to not wish upon anyone: enemy or stranger. The phrase uttered as an afterthought and carelessly said, forgetting the suggestion it confers upon the other party in the equation. Unless, of course, you really do think they'd had it coming.

It's a nice thought otherwise, as opposed to the other notions it ignores which are just as plausible: accident, mistake or simply plain dumb luck. Simply a random act of gods or goddess or plain nature happening which is why the grace of god, is the preferred concept. This of course begs the question, or should, about the workings of said grace and of its occasionally fickle the nature. Should said grace offer its favor upon one side, does it then conversely imply or mean clear disfavor upon the opposite side?

It asks or should a secondary question as well. The question being what has caused the city and her populace to have earned the disfavor of one on high if the claim to grace cannot be had? Does this thus surely mean it must be the opposite then, meaning disgrace? A disfavor perhaps unearned, if not clearly explained leading straight towards a trial without charges or proper prosecution whose simply skipping right ahead to the judgment phase. Is it no wonder then when there's a collective turn away from a being or concept constructed as described? How there should then be a seeking of alternatives away from these all powerful beings who'd pronounce such sentence upon the city without commutation or consideration for circumstances perhaps small and unavoidable; a mistake, a misstep after all.

Left graceless along the trip into the great unknown.

Fives

Five years gone now the papers say. Five years gone. Whether anyone's counting or not as the clock ticks through in time with the movie montage ripping calendar pages off of the wall. Five years down and the city is none the better for it. But then, five years passed is not as long a period as it sounds. Not as long as time goes or can be measured or divided, and yet, and yet it's time passed. A marker for having moved on and a point to reference when perhaps one has not followed the imploration to get past it or some such trite shit.

A woman down from the north knows it's August by the heat and the sweat which holds a continuous clinging path along every part of her body. She's come down with a group to reclaim things which have been lost, to rebuild, to help. But also to assuage guilt built by the passivity in watching the drama on CNN and silently thinking how the city had deserved it, while publicly acknowledging the shame of it all. She feels a bit of embarrassment for having wished ill at a city and her populace from across the TV screen. For the schadenfruede momentarily embraced and offered up with a prayer to boot given thanks for the misfortune skipping over her.

It's an apology no one will hear which is alright. It was never the primary purpose anyway. She'd come down to help and maybe for some other reasons all her own. Some known and confessed to and others perhaps not so much with more underneath lying in a layer of her subconsciousness close enough to still feel them nudge and tug at the edges on occasion. Whatever the reason, here she was in the August heat as sirens intercede from off in the distance screaming emergency through all of the other far off sounds shattering the stillness here where she sits. She wonders how much more the city and its populace can take. There lies a stillness minus any of the incidental noises most common to a living city. Like the buzzing of bugs or chatter of birds, a bark of dogs or anything like it. It's taken some getting used to. She'd taken some time to even recognize how the underlying hum of life was missing from these parts.

She sits down on the remains of a chair still sturdy enough to hold her. She presses the heel of her hand against her brow glancing up at the relentless sun while raising her constant companion of bottled water to her lips to take a quick sip. She sighs, glad for the work and the heat to help keep her mind from all the things and thoughts she expressly came down here to get away from after all. She'll soon continue on with the reclamation project here similar in its likeness to her own attempted salvaging of self as her own private penance. She offers herself up to the heat and sun of August in New Orleans like they are the embodiment of some ancient god or goddess from whom she might display this good deed here of her own rebuilding. It is an offer she makes without asking or wishing for any exchange for this deed and thus increasing her chances for the same.

Reparations to the city, a piece at a time as a blind metaphor for rebuilding herself though it's not the descriptive she'd have chosen or the narrative tact she'd take if she should care to explain it. Her motivation is not so simple as to be boiled down to one good solid reason versus a thousand smaller ones quickly adding up before demanding some form of action on her part and this is the action completed.

She cannot help but think of the mark of time. The fifth anniversary of the most destructive hurricane in recent memory making this a most unhappy anniversary for the city. A mostly joyless and grim black mark upon the calendar as a reminder of things lost and never to be recovered. Intangible things like futures and pasts. An entire course of history changed. The entire course of 600,000 lives altered in hours. The stamp of time smudged and imperfect forever more quoth the pelican, sayeth the disillusioned, the bitter and failed upon. But fuck, what a morose thought and one she doesn't feel qualified to have as an interloper upon the scene. She a stranger descended to stake her claim upon the storm ravaged city more akin to a vulture and carrion than anything else.

Large parts of the city still lay fallow and empty if dry and have become forgotten the farther receded from the front pages the story has receded in the past five years. Someone declared the recovery as fact and then it became so. Then it became old news which is the worst kind of news in America. All is well; we built a memorial to the disaster. We declared victory and moved on. It is oh so very American of us all and still the city is an empty shell of itself.

Can it be recovered if it'll never be the same again, never be whole? A lost identity even if it might be for the better, inviting the cliché about yesterday's gone. Then there's the other little chestnut about how the only constant is change with the additional fallacy of how change is always for the better, piling on the clichés. Such useless unhelpful bullshit as time marched on and if our luck holds we will find a scratch or two of a brilliantly summarized paragraph in some obscure history text.

The Gulf is bleeding and has been for nearly five months now. Spewing black out into the blue of the Gulf like the anger of undersea gods letting their displeasure be known. Another strike at the city, another attempted murder or mercy kill unknown. It makes the northern woman wonder what the city could have done to invoke such blatant attempts against her, her kith and kin. The blue of the Gulf is smeared with stains and streaks of uncounted barrels of black oil to mar her surface. The slick spreads as the government and the corporation argue over how many thousands of gallons the widening, thickening slick contains. A seemingly moot point to those increasingly encroached upon at its ever growing and encroaching edges.

Man paid the gods no heed; offered no respect in another attempt at thwarting them and nature herself built upon overconfidence and miscalculation of epic proportions.

It is one interpretation of the signs. One way they can be read if one has a care to but only if the intent is on reading things in an apocalyptic fashion. A choice made to believe the possibility of once true gods who now punish the city and her inhabitants for too many good times rolled. A long held but

The answer is found in a more ancient concept, though seldom employed policy. It was an offence the Greeks once considered the greatest one which could be committed before the gods and the world. They labeled it hubris and the punishments for this crime were often both terrible and legendary in equal doses. It makes you wonder if the gods hate the populace here in this most haunted land. Jealous of the resiliency of this city upon a curve along the ancient river along its breadth and power flowing in parts through the city and giving her its resolve.

The river, ancient itself and home to The Man of The Waters, is evidence of things which have been here longer and will be here long after the world has passed beyond the point where those here are but a small footnote preserved in history books should they be written. But the river and the skies and even the land itself begrudge the city its stubborn existence. Humanity's attempt to tame all of these so very ancient things as if they'd not a care at all for the things done to them or in their name and most likely against them. Ignoring their warnings as they shift and assail against the efforts made no matter how small or seemingly inconsequential. Taming attempts leading directly from hubris, from the continued generous allowance for kidding ourselves into thinking we're the masters of the world, when we clearly are not and it shall be our undoing.

It matters naught, or very little, any of the reasons which could be offered against the simple facts and the ample evidence of the events as they have come to pass and roost over the city. The winds blew, the waters rose and now the oil runs and the Gulf burns with fire at night like a false sun setting on the waters. It leaves one to wonder it these are not signs of the apocalypse or evidence of a god or gods who hate.

Little wonder then how so many have turned themselves against the gods or forgotten them in pursuit of newer gods, like progress and science. Good gods all, though not nearly as old or powerful in a place so clearly adjacent to all of the other parts of the wide wild world.

The northern woman never had much time for a god of any faith, sect, slant or denomination before this. After viewing the destruction wrought here, she's found it even harder to embrace the concept of a just and loving god compared against the evidence of this event. The hurricane's aftermath a philosophical argument made real if you will. Comfort is found then, if it's to be found at all, in more ancient concepts dating back a thousand years or so. They've been discounted and called myth now without consideration in this our information age, our enlightened age but maybe they were more correct back then than we are now.

Thin Lines

It's the third day of the ten she'd promised and already the work has taken its toll upon her previous good intentions to an extent she's not so sure this was ever a good idea. It's a hard argument to dispute versus how there's been so little offered up as reward compared to all their efforts made to alter the situation. So much is still left to be done. She wonders if ever it will be finished. She feels guiltily about the silent skepticism allowing for the negative possibility and shakes her head at the shame of it all. Still, she and her group can say they've done their part now and now they too are citizens of this city even as they leave her as they've always found her before. Then leaving the city and their dirty little secret sins behind with an ever so mischievous smile for parts far flung and unknown.

She wonders why the bother, to what end do they all come down here and work. 'Recovery,' is the known goal even if no one exactly knows what the definition might be or looks like for that matter. Recovery cannot be seen from here, not presently, and perhaps not for a long time despite the investiture of time and energy of indeterminable amounts. She secretly pines for the end of her commitment and a return to normalcy which she even manages to think without a trace of irony. A little pang of guilt at this as she returns to face a house with a red X painted on it, like so many others in a stricken part of the city. It's a little farther from the spots which received all of the press and still damaged all the same. Water, water everywhere, she thinks noting the descending lines marking the house and the departure of the waters. She's channeling Coleridge's 'Mariner' now, thinking back to the images transmitted by TV for the world to see the harm done when water's allowed to go where it will, whither it wants, unchecked and unchallenged.

Salvage and recovery of anything usable has become a new booming business in the city. The demand for the parts from the destroyed houses to be used in the rebuild of the houses left behind to be saved. Irreplaceable parts of houses and buildings dating back a hundred years or more in a direct tie to the city's past and history. A cannibalization feasting on the old to rebirth the 'new;' and all a relative term in a city as old as New Orleans.

The northern woman enters back into a house with the familiar red X painted on the front indicating it had been searched and found lacking in victims without mention of survivors. She always ponders this and wonders briefly if survivors were assumed and if so, scattered to which corner of the country could ever return. She moves into the back room of the cottage style house which sits between two of the traditional shotgun houses which are ubiquitous throughout all of the city's neighborhoods.

Inside the house it's even more still than outside. She cannot even hear the outside or the other people working with her a room or two away except for the occasional scrape of a chair or the crash of trash as it's thrown out of the windows or doors to the front and taken by another group to the truck hauling the debris away.

She moves deeper into the cottage style house denoting the overwhelming smell of mold and stale mud and the remains of water permeating everything. It's a reminder she's forgot to put her mask on, normally a requirement to enter these buildings. The mask is at her neck where she's pulled it down upon her exit to take a break. She lifts it up to cover her nose and mouth as she returns to work. She's digging through cabinets in the remains of the kitchen, minus the already long gone refrigerator which had left its putrid stench of rotted foods behind as a permanent haunt. The cottage is soon to have its destruction completed. Finally wiped from the earthly plane as another place marked by a sidewalk soon leading up to nothing, the lone sign anything other than emptiness was ever here prior. Before long the grass will rises up to heights which will hide even these remains to further match its departed neighbors throughout the area.

The haunting grassed over concrete pads are hard to see anymore let alone the steps up to houses no longer there. Washed away or torn down unknown and not much matter really one way or the other. Unknowns all and marks of what used to be and, with a borrow of a local phrase; 'aint dere no more.'

Going about the job of cleaning, she allows herself to get lost in its repetitive nature as she moves back and forth from the kitchen to front door to place debris in one pile and possibly recoverable parts in other piles. A hammer sways in its loop in the belt along her hips as she makes her way back and forth inside the house and out.

With the cabinets done, her gloved hands work at the drawers beneath until finding one which is resistant to her efforts to open from the warping sustained from the water damage. It's what she tells herself now and will seem quaint and quite naïve later after all of the things opening the drawer leads to. For now, the resistant drawer requires the claw of her hammer to loose the drawer and sends it flying along with her in a crash to the floor.

The northern woman sits up laughing a little bit at the outburst of the drawer which had flattened her straight on to her ass in an undignified manner. She surveys about her and discovers something odd lying in the debris of the resistant to open drawer. Lying face down on the silt covered floor she spies a curious copy of a dog eared paperback book she'd missed somehow. She turns it over and sees it has fallen open to pages 126 and 127.

She turns the book over to read its front cover and is surprised to see it's a copy of that old Stoker book smeared with mud and bloated from the waters with a smell of wet earth and stale river waters receded. Its pages are torn and frayed, its spine broken in more than one place, though she soon discovers it seems to have an unnatural predilection or perhaps affinity for pages 126 and 127. A habit she will come to learn is both persistent and determined.

She looks at those persistent pages and notes where a strongly emphasized quote underlined in red by the previous owner resides on page 127. The northern woman hasn't read this book since college after having seen the Frank Langella movie on TV in the early a.m. one night when she couldn't sleep combined with taking a Goth Lit class with too much Edgar Allan Poe on its syllabus.

She picks up the book to the ever fateful and near always face-up and insistent page 126 and 127 to read the strongly emphasized quote underlined repeatedly in red ink. She's actually quite familiar with the quote which speaks of death and the occasionally beneficent mood offered some small relief from its scarier aspects. A strange, if pertinent quote which has the northern woman quickly scanning the book to see what other patterns she might discover in the selections chosen and emphasized. Curious for whatever clues they might offer to the mystery of this book tucked away here with whatever else might be tucked away waiting discovery.

She quickly thumbs through the book to find out its other secrets but they provide no further insight than the bad penny line demanding attention with its blatant display of page 126 and127. The finding of the old Stoker book seemingly innocuous except for the pestering 'pay attention to me' quote was fast giving rise to her curiosity. It has her wondering which in turn causes her to rise and seek out what else she might find still in some semblance of salvageability. She searches for any kin left with the book and its underlined and marked passages.

She doesn't know it then and won't rightly understand it until it's much too late, as is true in any good horror story told. But with the discovery of the Stoker book and the subsequent decision to explore further she's crossed a line unseen between this world and whatever's next. And this is the very last moment when turning back is still an option for her.

It's a thin line. Thinner than is most commonly thought or considered and too easily crossed. Just one slip and it's already behind her. It happens when she wasn't looking or when she'd looked the other way. In a moment when she'd not been paying attention. A fatal lapse and no decision made to do so. The line is passed before she knew she'd done it. It's done with good intentions and bad thoughts, and it's done in small decisions and large and sometimes no decision whatsoever. A Rubiconic moment in the blink, or less, of an eye. One simple draw of breath and past it to the point of too late and too little, no effort at all really. Everyday small steps taken or large strides as it makes no matter whether it's done on purpose or by careless mistake. The reasoning or the happenstance is of no consequence in the step across because the line bears no definitives nor cares for the trifles of definitions in languages it does not communicate in or understand. Luckily, it's only surprising the first time and forever after it's as clear as a thing can be. So clear she wonders how it could ever have ever been missed in the first place.

A thin line too easily crossed with one little slip and no full step required and not what it perhaps should feel like. It seems how it ought to carry a heavier gravitas to the moment at a minimum. The second step is even less remarkable by comparison to the first. The first after all where one expects the enormity of it all too really press its full weight upon a person. The second foot doesn't even drag a toe as it too slips past the thin line too and not such the hard task previously envisioned.

She pockets the book for later when she's back on her bunk to read until lights out is called. There she's stealing away with a flashlight under the covers like when she was a little girl or harking back to her college days and late nights of trying to scare the hell out of each other with classic horror movies. A good scare is what she's after as she begins the classic text. A little something to take her mind off of the real horror in full display all around her project of reclamation.

She reads until her eyes struggle to stay open and then reads some more until she finally capitulates to the sandman and falls asleep with the Stoker book in hand. Her thumb stuck in its pages until it slips when she shifts in her sleep and the book falls to her side open to pages 126 and 127. Her hand will soon to follow to help keep the page open.

Nyctophobia

She's walking through the Quarter late evening or early morning. The time's irrelevant because it's an hour in the Quarter which is indistinguishable from either definition or description of time. She's walking home from her shift behind the bar when something grabs her from out of the dark, er, correction, the dark itself suddenly grabs her.

Strong, so very strong and not as cold as you might think. There's a stale warmth to it, especially in its breath past rotted teeth and on a fetid tongue with gore still slicked up in its mustache covered lip.

Throttles her. No other word for it. Throttles her so she knows there is no mercy to be had or any which will be offered. At the same time, it communicates how this particular experience will be neither quick nor slow. These are measures which have no meaning in the vein the dark will be working in. Its motif is pain and she is to be its masterpiece.

Then the dark takes her within its folds into a much darker place. Darker than anything she's previously known or thought could be possible. Simply seeming only to let one know such places do in fact exist and should not be treaded upon or near by the living kind.

His hands upon her in a sick form of caress or a search for the perfect hold. She's uncertain which or what the dark thinks of it. It's enfolding her within its so very long arms bringing forth a whimper from her, a subdued sob she wishes for it not to hear. The hands find their purchase as the too long arms encircle and entrap her body like coiled serpents in a perverse rendering of what could be mistaken for a lover's embrace.

A snap, an ugly snap, which she realizes represents something fairly vital of hers making this sound even as she goes slack. A horrible word to describe the loss of the ability to feel one's own self and body. The dark has broken her neck and paralyzed her and now it's solely the dark holding her upright, bringing her whimper up a notch to a small cry. A sob at her lips low and mournful, tears being the last thing left which she can actually control. She allows them to fall freely knowing they're the last she'll ever shed.

His tongue is everywhere from her neck down to her breasts scratching like sandpaper or the sensation of a cat's tongue though far more unpleasant as it moves along her sensitive skin. It's disgusting, revolting and all she wants to do is get away which is the one thing the dark has insured she cannot do and it makes her want to scream though she knows there isn't anyone to hear her.

It lingers at her neck in a classic vampire strike pose with its tongue playing its rancid way across her tender exposed flesh with his sharp teeth nipping.

A cold steel blade slides across her hip and inside the seam of her jeans followed by the mean hiss of steel and fabric. The dark jerks its arm and the steel rips the jeans off of her. Harsh impossibly long fingers reach out from very large hands to probe unfriendly into her. They penetrate rudely and uninvited in concert with the sharp points stabbing into her neck. Four points of invasion as her life's blood spews forth, her eyes fluttering as darkness descends.

And now you know the why behind the fear of the dark. The darkness holds death there, waiting at every turn and around every corner. It begs a healthy respect from those traipsing about out on its edges because the dark is home to the scariest things after all. And the scariest things are the reason, of course, why the dark has the reputation it does after all.

Sirens scream off somewhere in the distance like a thousand clichés before them. The colored lights bouncing off of the slicked pavement and the too closed in walls of this narrowed section of street and city. People are gathered at the periphery, unofficially marking off the area around the paramedics who are working feverishly over a hapless victim who lies in the street. Blood runs all about her to catch in her clothes, her hair and then the cobblestones.

A mask is placed over her nose and mouth as the EMTs surrounding her double their numbers and effort as the desperate struggle continues its appointed path. Orders are given, the vitals monitored and status listed. Their tone masks their thoughts but not very well for what they know. They knew it from the moment of arrival. There was little chance, almost none at all, but they are trained to ignore the odds, to increase the odds, to fight the odds and tell them to fuck off. It's a pure form of defiance in flying against the odds. It's a heroic moment in a long chain, even if it's all destined to be for naught as the damage is too much. The body has lain too long in the cold dank street and the person behind the mask has already made her acceptance speech. There's only so much more damming against the inevitable tide which can be done. These beautiful people knew it from the moment they stepped up to the challenge and to their credit they never blinked or hesitated even if they never really believed anything could be changed at all in this instance. The fight was rigged from the start, always is. Things can only be delayed for so long before it must be called quits and the debts paid off.

She finds herself both looking up at them and looking down at the whole scene, a truly unique points of view and a situation rarely afforded and this one but briefly. It takes a moment before she realizes she's in the scene and she's above the scene and whether up or down, she tries to tell the EMT's to stay their effort, to not bother. She's already half gone and slipping further by the moment. The odds hadn't been stacked in their favor long before they got to her and they slide exorbitantly against them with every tick of the clock whether any can hear it or not. She can hear the ticking. She hears it clearly even as it begins to fade away from her with its lessening meaning with every pass, every strike at sixty as time spins on in its merry way round the dial.

The fight continues as blood works its way up from deep within her body and wrestles its way up into her throat until it spews forth and into the mask on her face. The EMTs clear the mask from her and move to clear her mouth and throat but it's an effort which is met with failure as one last clear breath escapes and the body settles to the pavement permanently.

They make the call by a glance at their watches and the darkest part of night claims yet another to its embrace as the world continues on in its spin. Sirens are silenced. They're use reserved solely for the living and there is no longer any hurry or need for their mournful notice now that a different destination is called for than was previously hoped. Yellow tape is extended between the crowd and the body, calls are made, a few questions are asked, but there are no answers forthcoming nor will there be. This case is destined for the Jane Doe files on their pass through to cold case and the dust of the forgotten and long ago.

Wait.

Wait, this is not her death. This, these, are not her memories. These are not her last moments or thoughts. Nothing within this belongs to her. These are not her moments and this is not how her life played out. Pardon is not played out, yet. She swats away the melancholic faint tune buzzing at her ear. She wants to scream; feels the need to shout to make herself heard above the cacophony, above the relentless din invading. To rail against the overwhelming unreal memory, an unowned thought which is not hers, cannot be hers, which she wishes desperately for to not be. It's some very frighteningly real nightmare instead she decides, preferring this thought above all others. Otherwise it feels all too real. It clings to her as something belonging to her, something all her own despite all of the logical reasons how it cannot be. How it cannot exist beyond the realm of dreams and fantasy or insanity. If she were not so shaken she would feel more certain, more sure about the assertation. She could make a definitive stand and declare against it with the simple truth of her being alive and well. She could offer this up as her evidence against this lingering scenario against and within her person like a seductive grace were it not so disturbing.

The sunrise chases the sound of the flat line from her mind and she's mildly surprised to find herself awake and alive upon her small pallet surrounded by the detritus of living. She stares in wonder at the treasures of old food containers, scattered newspapers, clothes washed and not strewn about. She hears the sound of birds, the sound of the world returning to her in all of its glories great and small and all the proofs of life surrounding and informing her existence, her life. Such small pleasures to rejoice in for what they offer or convey to her. The wonders which are always there but only the truly awakened can see, and see them she does in all of their varieties and details. 'Proof of life,' she shouts to the skies and to the greater gods if only they would hear her once, this one time, but no god answers her. There is simply the silence, the eerie silence from all of the stillness lying around her in this deserted patch of city.

She sits up in her bunk with a start waking from the nightmare within the nightmare with the Stoker book stumbling from her side and to the floor. She'd fallen asleep with the damned book in her hand. She sees as she bends over to pick it up how it's slightly dented now from where her fingers had dug into the softened paper of the book in the midst of her nightmare.

She laughs at herself, a nervous little laugh of relief, gratitude to find the sun again, to feel its welcoming warmth on her face and skin to drive away the distaste from last night.

She convinces herself with her ability to rise and greet the sun as sufficient evidence for a proof of life and a refutation of any dispute against it.

She pads over to the communal sink and pours herself some of the precious bottled water to splash against her face as another shock to drive away the darkness from last night from every last corner where it might have rooted into her. She blames the damn Stoker book for giving her the nightmares. It's what she gets for an overactive imagination and a wish for a good scare within the city limits of the most haunted city in America (at least according to its own propaganda). It was her own damn fault and the reason for her own little nervous laugh at her own hubris as she appreciated the irony after her vitriol against the drillers in the Gulf not so long ago. An irony most appropriately delivered.

Still, the dream and the book have her recall something she learned in some gonzo pseudo class not entirely or exactly sanctioned by the university way back when. The class something about psychogeography and its tenets or properties. The combination of principles from psychology and geography and applied to this place, combined again with her own troubled thoughts which are the same ones which had driven her away from her home and down to this place. She's somehow mixed them together to produce the terrors which had visited her last night. Explanations which all sound fairly reasonable, plausible even though leaving her to wonder why she still feels a creep of cold up and down her spine and a breath at her neck which she'll try to shake free of for the rest of the day.

The Rise Up

What in the hell is all this knocking about now? The woman most recently been named thinks out loud as she attempts to rise from a very deep sleep wondering how long she'd been out anyways. It's hard to keep track of time these days when it held so little meaning or sway over her not including however long the sleep had been.

The rise up is unpleasant for many reasons. It starts with the rather serious desire to not be doing it at all and followed closely by the protest of long unused muscles and bones protesting against the exercise there of and against their own will to boot like the remnants of a wicked hangover. Some Jack will stand as the cure for what ails her with the trickster element of how she still needs to rise up to claim the relief as well. Ah cruel bitch that irony is and unsympathetic to her plight as well.

She realizes the passage of nearly five years in her slumber from a drifting newspaper landed at her feet as if thrown from an unseen paperboy with perfect aim and appreciation for the moment. She picks up the tattered page reading the headline and the date. She's momentarily surprised at the passage of time, thinking to herself, my my but how time does fly but where to and why in such a hurry? Where does it have to be for it to move as quickly as it does?

Distraction is still her most common affliction in this state of in-between. She notes how it has reached a level of consciousness which she has not yet attained, way ahead of her once more, taking her focus off of the reason for her here standing. The disturbance to her rest, the call to rise up and offer an answer to the caller momentarily lost in the absorption of the contemplation of time and its varied vagrant ways.

Pesky, pesky poking about, this damned woman who seems compelled to disturb her rest now. Poking and prodding, and knocking about her things forgotten and left behind. She seeks, it seems, to steal her death, to take her very personal thing and make it her own. This is a very dangerous dip into the deep, fertile and mysterious pond of be careful if ever there was a toe inserted into a pool of water to gauge its temperature kind of a thing. The Haunt doesn't wish to rise but that woman seems to not understand the central rule, the guiding principle behind her, simply missing the point. The woman seems insistent on persisting in her course, unable to find the ability to leave things be, near begging from the haunt's perspective, to discover the consequence of the cliché of her actions. She will come to understand the lone rule and experience the Haunt's form of justice soon and up close. The woman will understand the dictate of non-toleration with the retribution called for. The Haunt will be the consequence, but luckily she's the last one.

Given name now, so named and called forth and none too pleased about it. She'll be less so once she sees the muck about of some intruder traipsing through her left behinds. Some snoop who seems unwilling to let well enough alone, a person unheedful of deeds done and consequences which must be met and meted out. Someone who must be taught how there are repercussion for such transgressions made.

Time to go out and prowl the night streets of her city, to put the fright back into those who would seek to do harm to her city. To those who've forgotten to heed her edict, those who've forgotten or willfully ignored the statutes against disturbing the dead and one northern woman in particular. Beware the darkness sweetheart. In darkness there is death and this haunt is at perfect home now within the embrace of night. She has become the darkness.

She slips into her unexercised role too long left to linger, glad to see it still fits her, glad it's still all hers like she never left it. She's determined to show the woman what her rage felt like, what the true meaning was behind the phrase 'fear of the dark.' She's much pleased with the idea of such as a just punishment for the woman's daring to disturb her rest. Give the interloper an example of the Haunt's activity, as a stark contrast to how it might be scribbled across whatever pages were left behind her. It was careless of her to do so she now knows, to have left those scattered about, but nothing for it now, nothing to be done about it directly.

Well Miss Busy Bee was in for a nasty surprise. A surfeit of punishment and pain which she, the Haunt called, had in stored reserves and felt very suddenly, generously like sharing. Rage for rage is the gift she's been given and the source for all of her great strength, all of her power when she stops in her tracks with another better thought in mind. A fit turnabout for the northern woman, a consequence she could not possibly anticipate or see coming. An indirect action, a sleight of hand if you will, if you'll allow. An idea the Haunt, as the northern woman had called her, liked so much now. She would give the northern woman an example of her defense of the city she called home and her creed without compromise. She would not tolerate in her city which she defended with extreme prejudice.

She turns to her hunt dragging her tenuous link to the northern woman along with and over her shoulder like a schoolbag. She reaches into her dreams to slip through the cracks the in-between affords her, combined with the woman's own fevered pursuit of her over these pages. Her near trademarked crooked smile crosses her lips and her tongue darts along the edges of her teeth hungry and eager now for any victim crossing her path, for any small misbehavior which meets her criteria for punishment.

Happily in her city, in this city particularly, these endeavors do not take long before they're encountered which is all the better as she was piss poor at patience despite the gift of so many years to her passing without touching her. She's moved back to her happier hunting fields, the old stomping grounds of her previous story with memories everywhere as she can no longer forget a damned thing anymore. She shakes the distraction when she spots what she's looking for a short distance away. She makes a quick and satisfying kill of an interloper crossing into her territory without permission, with bad intentions in his heart which she discovers after taking a bite of it.

She thanks the city for providing such a satisfying meal, for so quickly answering her call so she might fulfill her role within the societal chain. She appreciates the added bonus of this person's status so mimicking the bothersome northern woman and giving the haunt a momentary satisfaction of having dealt with her - at least by proxy for now.

For all of her quickness she'd rather made a mess of it. Too excited she guesses at her return to action, the invigoration of the exercise of her power and raw strength. She's still a little surprised at how it's grown over the last five years, unaware prior to this how she had the power to do what she has done and how a body could be literally torn apart piecemeal.

She stands a little shocked at the raw brute strength she now owns as she looks over the recent murder she's still ankle deep in. She's looking down at the remains with blood and gore still on her hands, the viscera of the body torn apart as she looks at her hands with their new and unexpected hideous strength. She's surprised once more by the details of this existence of hers here in the in-between. It seems it will never stop being full of surprises. Surprises like the strange mournful metallic notes she swears she can hear riding along lazily on the air as they're sing-songing their way about the Quarter to permeate the city. A little chill runs along the nape of her neck which causes the hairs there to stand on end telling her with no uncertainty she's no longer alone here. She raises her head to look about for the source but sees not a soul despite the faint song on the wind and the distinct sense of someone's eyes upon her for a moment. A faint 'damn girl,' vocalized in her ear spikes the chill straight down her spine making her leave this spot post haste to find some light some distance, from the source of the scare. Even frights can have enough sense to not mess with anything which can give them a spook; like the one currently causing the primitive danger danger signal deep within her lizard brain saying 'run fool, run.' And run she does, trying to get as much distance as possible from the haunting mournful tune.

Daylight

The relief of daylight greets her as she wakes from the pull of the terrors of the night before with the too vivid dream of that damned haunting woman still clinging to her. She feels like vomiting anything she might have in her stomach but luckily there's nothing there. Still, another day and another dream from the night before with the dark haunt still knocking about the inside of her skull come the morning and none too subtlety either. The Haunt seems to be growing in strength with each additional night and its subsequent frights becoming somehow more real to her as if the scary woman really existed. The northern woman could appreciate the statement ironically and with a groan like a lame one-liner from the files of wasn't what you were hoping for after all. And she's not at all glad about the blurring of fact and fiction and still without an ounce of proof of any kind for a story starting at unbelievable.

She sits up feeling every single ache large and small throughout her entire body sore beyond the simple explanation of the previous day's work done. She's hanging her head in her hands like she went on a bender last night and would be a long time recovering from it. She raises her hands high above her head in a long luxurious stretch blowing out a long satisfied breath. It's on their descent when she notices how they're curiously stained dark with a rust color especially at fingertip and under her fingernails. She doesn't recognize this color as anything familiar and has no clue as to its arrival there upon her hands.

She gets up to go and wash the strange discoloring away, stumbling over her yellow construction boots hastily cast aside the night before. She bends down to move them out of the way only to discover how they too are marked with the same type and color of stains matching what's on her hands and under her fingernails. Her kicked off jeans are similarly imbued with the rust like color as is her white tank top when she finds it with the edges of its waist and sides torn to shreds and the tank all but rendered unwearable.

Puzzling, she thinks as she picks up the pieces, the remnants, of her clothes and throws them away, even the jeans so coated with the unidentified staining material as to be stiff and unbendable back into a resemblance of a flat pair for even legendary Herculean strength. She's no recollection of ever having left her little bunk, though she does have an internal exhilaration deep down and unexplained and curiously, for her, no interest in exploring or investigating satisfied with it as it is.

She'll try hard to tell herself this moving forward, to convince herself of this even when she closes her eyes and lets her mind wander and it reveals some frightening things to her which she wishes to dismiss as nightmares. She rather prefers this idea, chalked up to an overactive imagination fed by the old Stoker book and her presence in this still eerie city. She wants very badly to believe this, has to convince herself of the truth of this version of events because the other options are more horrible to contemplate than the idea of nightmares. The other options for her are insanity itself or that the nightmares are real as evidenced by the stains on her clothes. The stains and the memories are her truth, and she's already lost and unable to save her soul.

She thinks to scream, how a scream would be monumentally helpful for her here for stress relief if nothing else. Her entire body shakes with the suppressed scream. Shaking violently as she wishes hard for the scream to burst forth though no sound rises in her throat to offer up to the wild winds. She's left wishing hard for a scream to shatter the illusion she's trapped in or to protest against her new reality if it's what's to become of her. To rage like a long ago poem, to rage against it so this new reality will at least know she did not go along willingly. Her entire person bounces between the hot anger of the nightmare world of her dreams which have apparently spilled into a very real reality. Deep sorrow begins to fill her person at every level of her being and in every instance of her having been. It tastes bitter in her mouth from the back of her tongue all the way to the front edges of her lips. It's wholly invasive and nastily repugnant and not at all like all those damned lying poets who'd written on it previously.

She returns for a moment to the idea of her going straight bat shit fucking insane. She turns it over in her mind wondering all the while if this is what insane feels like or if it's even identifiable by the person slipping over into the malady. She wonders if the descent into insanity is painful and abrupt, like a fall from a height followed by the oh so sudden stop at the end or if it's more like surrendering to water and slowly sinking beneath its surface until you're too deep to save yourself. Her other alternatives are equally depressing to contemplate. The options veer from her being locked into or lost within a nightmare versus some other horrific alternate reality. The only relief is how both hold out the possibility of her still escaping from either of them.

She has few scarce alternatives otherwise and all of them share the qualities of being solidly unpleasant to contemplate or consider. They fell into two primary categories. Adjectives both which one generally did not aspire to or seek out for themselves: insanity or murder. She's uncertain which of those two realities facing her is the worst or more damned of the two. She herself is caught now in an inability to distinguish, even if only for a small moment, the difference between the terrorized dream and reality, day from night and herself from itself.

Suddenly her decision to give the woman a name, to call her out by the same, didn't seem such the cute idea anymore. It didn't seem like the stroke of clever she'd congratulated herself for way back when. No longer the cutesy name given or used anymore the northern woman thought, simply the Haunt forever more as name for her adversary now with all due apologies to Mister Poe.

The northern woman continues her struggle versus the new reality twisted so as the Haunt had moved from simply stalking her dreams to now lingering into the proverbial cold light of day. Previously the part of the day long held and often told in the myths as the safest part for humans, the one advantage they'd over the supernatural. All exposed now as another damned lie by the Haunt in her most frightening aspect yet. The Haunt still tromping around in the northern woman's head in the waking world and threatening to transform this *relationship* into something else altogether much to the northern woman's dismay and great disbelief.

There's one clear point she does have to chalk up against any disbelief though she does try her hardest to ignore it. One very visceral and very real killing done and no matter anymore if it's from her dark and disturbing nightmare or her waking reality. The killing leads directly to her in the most obvious of ways marking her quite clearly as the perpetrator of said crime despite her refusal to accept it. She prefers still to blame this on that damned woman Haunt, who has escaped from her dreams and back out into the real world and then to make her complicit, an accomplice to the deed done.

She doesn't know how she knows this or why. More importantly why it doesn't horrify her more, coupled with her lack of any real remembrance of the *crimes*. It seems important to her she should recall something of the act other than the blood on her clothes and the memory of after the fact as she was currently experiencing.

The circumstantial evidence against her is stacked high as compared to her pleas of innocence. Evidence clearly upon her own betraying hands stained with the rust red colors. The traitorous digits which she wishes to deny as her own, to distance herself from and the possible actions they've committed. Whether or not of their own volition or by the command of the stalking and seemingly now ever present Haunt. The rusted red stains which permeate her clothes, her hands and her skin must be washed away before they permanently imbue deeper into her and down to her very soul. A 'black mark' on her permanent record as used to be said. The kind of mark you carry with you for the rest of your life and if you're famous or infamous - beyond it too.

Her own personal Mark of Cain if you're feeling biblical, but the view point doesn't matters much here. It's rendered transparently irrelevant by the real and viscous blood on her hands as evidence literally at arm's length. She holds her arms out to either side and away from her torso as she has no desire to have them close to her. She still wishes somehow to assess a certain amount of blame to them as if they are separate from her. If she keeps them away from her their deeds will not cling to her which she wishes hard for because she cannot stand to look at them anymore.

She keeps looking straight ahead for fear of discovering any more bloody clues about her. She rushes to the shower in a hurry to cleanse herself in more ways and meanings than the traditional reasons would grant. The shower's turned on to its hottest temperature, hotter than she can probably stand. This is okay by her as she wants to burn, knowing from some far off recess of her brain how this is a purifier, a means to cleanse herself. Scrubbing her body to a bright pinkish hue, the water turned to waste circling about her feet and ankles at the bottom of the shower. She silently hopes the river can take it from her to deposit all the way away and deep into the gulf with her hoping the waters don't mind.

She stays under the spray until the water finally turns from cold to frigid before finally surrendering to all of the new fantastic facets of all the fear she's experiencing. A new delight courtesy of her torment, the Haunt. She sinks to the far corner of the bath huddled naked with her forgiving arms wrapped about her. The tears descend, hard racking tears from down deep within and continuing until she's well past dry and exhausted though her still wet hair drips its last cold drops upon her toes.

First and with some difficulty, she convinces herself to rise up and slowly does. She's unaware of how long she'd stayed bunched like that, though judging by the pops and creaks which mark the protestation of her body as she uncurls and rises. It had been a rather lengthy stretch of time. She's probably not finished with the sorrowed portion of the event but simply out of tears as opposed to the much more positive spin of 'aint gonna cry no more.'

She's still feeling sorry for herself though. She's exhausted and spent from the twists and turns of the previous untold hours piled up and threatening to overwhelm her. She finds herself wishing for a small sliver, a small piece of relief from the pressures and confusion of her present state which she can cling to and tightly too, as if her life depended upon it.

She crawls towards her bunk seeking to slink beneath the pile of clothes lying there, thinking how they might serve her as a sanctuary however temporary or seemingly flimsy it might appear. Sleep though she begs for it, wishes for it to come and claim her, but it does not immediately seek her out. Seems outright uninterested in finding her for the longest time, no matter how damn hard she wishes for it now. Such sweet relief for her to be able to surrender to sleep and find it at least as long as it takes the Haunt to come find her in the night. Both arrive within minutes of each other in the early hours, right before the dawn.

Pandorium

Last night's nightmare has been put in a safe side place as she tries hard to conveniently forget the scare to make it easier to discount this way. The bright light of the sun unblocked by clouds beats down and heats her skin and burns away the fright of last night. She chides herself with a self-conscious laugh under her breathe about the Stoker book giving her a good scare. Thinking to herself how she should be a little too old for such things, if still a little glad too for the ability to still become a little frightened.

Today she appreciates the work if nothing else than for its ability to take her mind off the book and the nightmare. Unfortunately it's not to be for long as the northern woman's curiosity is piqued to capacity at the sight of the dresser in the bedroom. She tries to ignore it, tries to put it from her mind as she toils in other areas knowing how, except for the dresser, this house is almost finished in every sense or definition of the word. Ignoring it does not make it go away. It instead makes it grow like the insistently annoying scratch just out of reach; but this one isn't out of reach, this one could be satisfied, if only she would.

She finally gives in to the insatiability of her curiosity. She returns to go through the ruined dresser sunk and bended towards its missing leg but still generously describable as serviceable. One of the few pieces of furniture still existing in this household. She's not certain why she does this as it feels like some form of violation, a sacrilege if you will and still her curiosity is too strong to stop her now once started. It needs an explanation as to how this dresser arrived here mostly intact and usable if you weren't too picky about your décor when everything else is gone or in innumerable conditions best described as ranges of destroyed. She wonders if this is the dressers proper home or if it too is lost and now cast in a new and unfamiliar environment like so many throughout the city.

Every race and religion invokes warnings against disturbing the dead and their places of rest. The warnings seem to bear an especially closer scrutinization here in this most haunted city so recent on the heels of such tragedy, such pain. The perfect breeding grounds for things which will soon go bump in the night. She ignores these random thoughts and chases away doubt with a flick of her gloved hand as if she were clearing a cobweb from her face. She clears another drawer from this strangely intact and empty dresser with nothing to show for her efforts, but soon the northern woman will make a discovery to change her world. Until then, there's the mold, the dirt, the heat and one last chance for her to stop and catch herself and heed so many warnings.

The rest of the discovery waits for her in the last drawer, the bottom dresser drawer, the finalist in her searching. Inside, shifted into its fallen corner, she finds a small wooden box wrapped and shut tight by what she takes to be rubber bands but are actually a multi-colored collection of women's elastic bands used to tie up ones hair which strikes her as so odd. An out of place find in a flooded city followed by a fleeting moment, a glimpse of Pandora and her own box not to be opened before she too was overwhelmed by curiosity and succumbed. Reason tells her this is foolishness but her brain refusing to believe in anything which smacked of irrationality. Her arrogance and ego leading her down a crooked path which she could see if she were to raise her eyes to their obviousness.

One last chance to exercise prudence, proper caution, but it's not to be.

She removes the dime store hair bands from around the box wondering if the owner of this is the same as of the old Stoker book. She pauses a moment to suck in a breath as she looks about her as if to firmly anchor herself in the present time and place. She then looks back down at the ordinary wood box steeling herself as she imagines what Pandora must have done with her own box. Her hands move over the cover of the box without lock or other means to further prevent the exploration of its contents. The wood is smooth and once well decorated with a map of the world beneath the grime and dirt collected on its surface. She's on her knees, feet behind her and against her rump with the box in her lap as her hand grabs a corner and raises the lid to find some random detritus and miscellanea, which means nothing to her now, but she'll know as talismans later. Beneath them are papers folded twice in half squares at the bottom of the box. She carefully removes the papers trying hard to not disturb the other contents. Her hands shake a bit for no obvious reason as she unfolds the pages and begins to read.

The words on the pages convey their menace and anger with their vivid black strokes. Always written in black ink on the paper no matter their coherency otherwise. The characters are drawn, are scratched into the pages and damn near leap off and strike out with a force. They seek provocation and find it in the first words as they seemingly slam against her conscience with their starkness, their naked power standing in defiance against all which might argue otherwise. "I will not tolerate," the protagonists sole statement of purpose or reason offered up as her raison d'être. Better yet, a battle cry and the sole explanation offered or given throughout the papers she finds within the drawer.

The original papers are incomplete and maddeningly random, cryptic and without order. Later she will discover this is true of all of the collected papers she will eventually find layered beneath the false bottom of the original drawer. The northern woman, the intruder, doesn't know about the other papers yet of course. She won't until after digging for them, hungry for more, searching for a greater explanation. She's scrabbling at the dresser and all of its drawers and walls as she searches for more of the work writ in a madwoman's hand. Convinced of her madness and wondering if the storm was the cause behind it like some warped creator god type myth.

If you go looking for things which are meant to be kept secret do not be surprised when you are punished for uncovering them. A philosophical if violent thought which escapes ready examination or efforts to quickly be tossed carelessly aside. These cannot be secrets, decides the person who has no authority over the text and words. Who has no ability to determine what they are one way or the other. They cannot be secrets she decides because they are in plain sight. She has conveniently forgot how she'd found them in the abandoned dresser. This becomes the next argument against secrets to be kept. The argument explains how they would not have been left behind had they been meant to be kept. No, lost is the word. The descriptor with which she can always invoke the immortal and irrevocable finders, keepers length of the law.

The northern woman finds within the madwoman's papers a combination manifesto and autobiography or a damned lie well told like any good fiction. Calling the gathered incoherent mass of scribbles 'papers' mind you, is a generous description of the collected mass which grows larger with each sweep and search conducted by the northern woman through the ruins.

The northern woman keeps sorting through the myriad of papers forgetting about the punishment offered for the curious cat, the metaphor escaping her as she digs through the ruined dresser. She starts through the rest of the room before rapidly expanding her search to the house and every one of its last lost and dark corners. She's determined to find every scrap which might be hidden, looking for whatever history this madwoman has left behind for her to read and devouring everything she finds. Left with nowhere else to search, she returns to the point back in the kitchen where she'd first found a part of the mystery. She reaches as far as she can into all of the cabinets and is rewarded for her perseverance when she grabs a corner of something shoved into the farthest back corner of a cabinet. She pulls it out to discover a small box with the last remains of the madwoman's scraps of paper.

The northern woman sits down to read and sort through the papers. She's shocked and unable to comprehend the sheer range of the rage behind the stroked words which give them so much more power with their strike against the paper. Her affliction grows in strength the deeper she delves into the papers and the more she reads in the pages. She finds herself sorting and resorting them backwards and forwards again and again and with one attempt at sideways to try and make sense of all of the impossible words she reads and the actions they hint at when they're not straight yelling them out loud. She struggles to put them into a collective narrative a plot line, something which can hint at some form of coherent story told. She is feeling strangely compelled to the sorting and reading and rereading mixed with an occasional resort to reshuffling the mass to see what it can yield.

She has a yellow legal pad to scratch her own thoughts onto. When it runs out she turns to scraps, then to napkins and lastly whatever other odd bits of paper she can find. She seeks to organize and write down her own feelings on the thoughts expressed to her en masse. She tears her notes from the pages and sets them about her on the floor in a circle. She numbers them in hope of keeping track of them, seeking to bring order to the chaos of the life lived out in the pages should she choose to believe the words written down.

She gathers up the papers she's written things down on and sets them in no particular order one atop the other in back into the same box she'd found the originals in. It's an imperfect filing system deemed sufficient for now. It seems more important to get the words down, to gather her thoughts however stream of consciousness they may be. She figures she'll always have the luxury of time later to reorganize and sort through the incoherency presented into a viable and workable narrative.

The northern woman sets the box of papers aside for a moment unwilling to believe the account offered in the pages. She chooses instead to believe they're a provocative fiction. She seeks to physically put the papers away so her brain might mark them in a bin to be forgotten. But her damned curiosity strikes again and she finds herself retrieving the box, pulling out the papers and rereading them. She begins again to sort the papers into a coherent narrative the best she can so she can then begin her search for information about the woman behind the words on the page in an effort to know if this woman is real. Her interest is unwaning and begging to be fed, demanding to know. She sorts the papers again trying to impose organization and coherency on the pile of scripts despite their resistance to the unwanted intrusion to every effort to assemble them. They seem to actively fight her as she tries to find the thread connecting them in the pure black rage, to assign them a timeline so she might correlate them to real things in the historically real timeline.

She's surprised at her choice of words, her frame of thought, to describe the situation facing her. A puzzling description setting her back in her organization as she contemplates and searches to find what she meant by the thought. She's trying to understand where it came from in so strange and random a fashion, normally so unlike her. It seems leaving the papers lie for a moment would be a wise course of action. The papers themselves find much satisfaction in this idea, seeming to shirk away from her and out of her immediate reach. They appear to be wishing hard for a return to their box and the darkness within where they'd be most comfortable and prefer or so she imagines.

The madwoman previously without name, whose presence burdens these papers, the northerly woman has discovered, has not been seen or heard from in the four years since the first year after the storm. The northern woman will soon discover how there's no record of the Haunt from before the storm either. Still her obsession drives her to discover any truth at all to the events described in the papers discovered. A true first person eye witness type account to history. But there's to be no hint, no clue, and no scrap of information to link the mysterious woman to anything other than the fevered imagination of a most haunted city. Its fevered citizenry lost amidst the chaos which followed the storm and the year of the madwoman's assumed activity afterwards.

Her infamy is confirmed in the killings which made the news. Confirmed and cross checked through the newspaper archives. Well, confirmed is a strong word for what is reported. Killings do make the news, especially strange ones. Once past the officially repressed details, some strangeness still leaks through and almost all of it's about a mystery woman she refers to as her Haunt. It's shorthand she's given for the words found between the lines writ on the papers and cross-referenced with anecdotes which she considers much less reliable. A generous description for the tales told. The stories have come from reluctant witnesses who mostly qualify as third or fourth person removed from any who actually bore witness to the Haunt. She was known to leave few alive in her wake to describe anything about her.

The northern woman is convinced her Haunt is caught somewhere in there in between the lines of the newspapers and the scrawled script. She feels like she almost has it. Almost has the thread of the narrative or at least enough to plot a line to carry the story of the madwoman through it, despite the obvious gaps and the maddening inconsistencies. The Haunt has double backed on herself in her descriptions or managed to have blended together their common enough elements as to make one as indistinguishable from the other.

It is long past time now since she was supposed to return home and yet here she still is lying motionless on her pallet, sleep having since abandoned her to her own devices, leaving her for good in an abandoned house in New Orleans. She's now caught in her own haunted land, captured or compelled, trapped or entranced in the words. The reason behind them of no matter, she can no longer tell the difference or define such distinctions as nuances have been lost to her. They've blurred into an obscurence which has removed or changed any useful references she may have once had or understood beyond recognition. She can still see but isn't able to identify what she sees with the increasingly nagging feeling she should be able to or at least once had been. It only adds to her thoughts of going insane, full circle if you will, or some Sisyphean wonder tale.

What she needs is proof of the madwoman to serve the dual purpose of disproving any descent on her part into insanity. More importantly, she thinks she knows where she can get some. Something more substantial than the generic newspaper clippings she's found so far. This is her reasoning when she decides to see if she can find the detective mentioned in the madwoman's papers. The detective, if real, was the lone tangible resource other than the city itself which she could cite as a solid reference point, a touchstone of reality to the unreality of the woman's papers. The northern woman believes if she can manage the trick of tracking the detective down, it alone would serve as proof. A touchstone at a minimum to the reality described in the papers or anything else which he might offer up and share with her would simply be bonus material for her.

Her search takes money and feminine wiles on at least one occasion as she attempts to vault the blue wall of silence to get anything tangible. Actionable is the word most commonly used in modern parlance. Her efforts are rewarded in a 'you didn't hear it from me, you were never here' type of action as a folded piece of paper is left on the table as she's still buttoning her shirt back up. She's been left alone in the small, chilly and dimly lit room once used way back when for interrogations. At least, it was what she'd been told prior to her personal up close interview bringing a wry smile to her face appreciative of the irony inherent in the descriptive.

She heads for the door nonchalantly picking up the folded piece of paper lying on the table looking discarded. She works to resist the temptation to open and read it before she's made her way back outside but is unable. Opening the paper she sees an address scrawled there in blue ink. An address in a part of the city she's vaguely familiar with but only recently. The address in a neighborhood which was right smack in the middle of the madwoman's hunting territory.

The northern woman finds the cop the Haunt had called 'capitaine,' tracking him down to his house courtesy of the passed on piece of paper. She finds him in a state of clear sobriety and cold coherency. His house and what she can see of it from over his shoulder and around his body blocking the doorway is neat, clean and organized.

It's made clear from the onset by his body language he's not going to move from the doorway and will not step outside and most certainly will not be inviting her into his home, His resentment at her presence clearly communicated. She's almost disappointed to find him in such a 'normal' state seemingly unperturbed, hale and healthy and apparently no longer obsessed with the Haunt of a woman which she presently is all wrapped up in. She surprises herself by resenting how he's apparently moved on and away from the Haunt squarely into the whole getting on with his life as she herself should probably be doing.

She introduces herself but he does not respond or even blink. She queries him about his presence in the madwoman's papers and other than a derisive snort, he does not confirm his presence, though he doesn't deny it either. She ogresses as he represents her lone slim cling at any hope of her being on the correct track here. He continues to answer with grunts and warnings, curtly quickly and rudely. There's at least one attempt to shut the door in her face when she mentions the dream of murder and mayhem. He looks at her a very long time with a rising anger in his features. His jaw working over whatever it is he's contemplating to say to her.

His response to her when it comes is a frightening and unworldly laugh followed with a final slam of the door on her. Between these two activities he offers her advice which is more like a warning about leaving well enough alone. To leave that damned woman alone if she had any sense at all. If she damn well knew what was good for her.

The advice echoes in her brain for a little while until she decides to stop this obsession of hers, this affliction before it turns to madness. She even manages to convince herself for a day or two she's accomplished this simple goal and still she'd not left when her group had. Still she had not gone and left things alone.

She stands in the same spot where she'd first discovered the box she'd been so successful in denying, or so she'd told herself. She stays unmoving in this same spot as the night gathers over and around the city by the bend in the eternal river. She swears for the briefest of moments, she can hear the hauntings of a few hundred years as they shift about the city they've come to call home. The words used are like another warning and likely to be defended as such and as well.

It's a notion to best be remembered when stepping blindly over the lines of territory marked out by others who would be only too happy to mark you as foreign and therefore prey ripe for the hunting.

She seeks to reassure herself by swearing promises to herself to stay for a few days more and this only to scratch the persistently current itch of curiosity. The promises and oaths sworn are false before they find breathe to finish expressing themselves. Before they fall in still birth from lips which do not believe the words they speak. It's the worst and highest form of crime to delude you with your own arguments and thoughts, a simple betrayal of the person to spin such tales, to tell such lies.

She should know better and were she truly a child of this city, she would. If she understood any one thing, any little thing at all about this city, she would not believe the deceitful words falling from her lips in promises empty and worthless. She would never have formed the thoughts, knowing from the start the waste of it all. The city has a way of getting in your blood, in your soul and your person, grabbing hold and never letting go. Whether you hate her or love her is unimportant. Hate her, she'll despise you and spit you out. But love her, love her, and she'll never, ever, let you go no matter how far you might move in time and space or throughout the world. She never, ever lets you go. Become obsessed with any part of her and you're truly lost. Lost forever and occasionally never to be seen nor heard from again except in the legends and urban myths with mythical mystical names to be forever attached to your deeds, true or not.

She opens the box again, the previous Pandoric moment passed by or more likely ignored at one's own peril. The lid has been carelessly tossed aside like all of her reasons, all of her thoughts on temporary stays. She's unaware of the consequence of this moment passed into the mists of history. Already long gone and beyond any reach of hands or turn rounds. No take backs as the child's game goes. This is the moment of no return and it passes unremarkably, lost before it's known to be gone or missing. Filed permanently under regrets or rue of day, a what if for a later day soon to come or potentially not at all. Tomorrow is nothing but a promise as had already been noticed and remarked upon. One last thought left though, a notice how there's never any way to get back or to undo what's been done.

Some things are not meant to be known or discovered, the ultimate example, if you will permit, of leaving sleeping dogs to lie. These things are better left lost where they fell to be forgotten or discarded with purpose. There's a reason they were left behind and thrown to the side of the world as it continued on its spin. There are some things which eagerly welcome the obscurity, embrace it as it were, which prefer to be left unsaid. They prefer their anonymity and being lost to the stream of history, forever unrecorded. Undiscovered, left alone, do not disturb, as if it could not be clearer. And yet sometimes things are poked and prodded about, needled beyond even mythical Penelope's patience. Then sometimes, some things will rise up to let you know the why of their being left behind. Why they'd chosen to be lost in the detritus of the past and the purpose behind it.

Simply a turn at speaking prophesies. A dangerous provocation and a word deliberately used in this manner, in this conjugation due to the lack of ability to explain what follows without this preface. She didn't know then how an ordinary person could speak prophesies or makes things true simply by speaking them out loud onto the multiverse. Had she known, she perhaps would have been more careful of the words spoken. If she had been even slightly aware of the consequences, she tells herself, her tongue would've spoken less courageously. She wouldn't have let it flap so freely. She, of course, learns later how her tongue hadn't exercised courage in the scenario. Instead, it had continuing on in its practiced recklessness and at such a pure level as to seemingly beg for the repercussions for the reckless daring done. But that was all ahead and unseen. Her casual flippancy could not be stopped or deterred and as is the universes want. The punishment came when it could be best understood and of a decidedly nasty variant.

Great Wide Open

Straight un-fucking believable how this damned northern woman still dares to call out the Haunt by name and too loudly, too carelessly shouting it to the heavens and hells too. Further tearing her rage open like a ragged wound. The damned woman who so blatantly and carelessly calls out her name at such volume as to wake every one of the damned and the dead with the call of her name carried forth on the winds of the city despite the warnings writ in the papers discovered.

This further disturbance is disappointing to her. It seems her previous warning has gone unheeded by the knockabout woman and requires some supplemental learning to reinforce the lesson of letting well enough alone. She decides to turn to her other tools, deciding to put a fright into the woman; to reinforce the point and what better way than the proverbial walk in one's shoes application idiom. Focus she demands. Focus on the damned northern woman who would not let her sleep. Who had not stopped poking her nose into things which did not want the intrusion or the notice for the damned woman who could not leave well enough alone despite ample warnings.

The Haunt steps off with a momentary twinge as she thinks for a short moment what a sight she must be in her old and torn blacks. They're splattered here and there with flecks of new blood from a fresh kill over the speckle of old blood still matted here and there. Especially nastily in her unkempt mess of black hair made darker now with the blood and viscera. 'Must be a fright,' she thinks to herself, laughing at the self-deprecating joke she's accidently made. She's hoping this has not caused other frights and haunts to be disappointed in her infringement on their specific territory and grant them cause to label her interloper or intruder. She didn't care to provide any causation for her removal by means most nefarious when she swears she hears something on the wind. She thinks for a moment what she hears is impossible and she tries to shake her head clear of the auditory phantom. She tries hard to ignore it as it fucks with her equilibrium while she attempts to walk away from it. Each step it pisses her off further until it strikes her clear and unmistakable. It is a metallic mournful tune which she's heard once before but is closer now and with the distinctive characteristic of closing in on her.

Recognizing the tune is a pleasant if unhelpful sensation and she wonders if there's some clever literary term to describe it and can think of none. No matter to her, she's not in any need of definitions or clever phraseology to appreciate and apply the terms. Rather a perverse form of pay it forward of a debt owed to the northern woman for having named her and then had dares to call her, all to casually disturbing her rest.

The northern woman dreads sleep now, as she probably should. Dreads what it might bring in the way of new terrors. Sleep seems like it's a signal or a sign of surrender to the Haunt who flits in and out of her dreams seemingly at will these nights. She is somehow making the northern woman feel responsible for the Haunt's actions which she is powerless to stop. Guilty conscience, she guesses, without a clue as to the why of the phrase's presence in her head over what she still assumes to be particularly vivid dreams.

The northern woman's tired enough after her long day of wanderings to make an attempt at falling asleep, thinking it should be easy enough to find. She's to be disappointed once more despite her protests direct to the sandman to grant her this respite. Exhaustion and the day's heat still cling to her as she lies on her pallet. Her shirt is covered with dirt and sweat clinging to her skin. Her bra is tossed carelessly off to the side offering only slight relief from the oppressive heat and humidity of a tropical land in the midst of August. Her jeans and boots still confine her skin within their fabric but she ignores their pleas for removal as anger rises at her inability to shut down and drift into the shelter of slumber. Perhaps the Sandman knows better than she and better remembers the nightmares from the night before. Better recalls the potential return of the Haunt who had roamed through, even if the northern woman has forgotten or blocked it from her mind presently.

The northern woman's brain keeps returning to the writings she'd discovered a few days before, the same ones she'd swore she wouldn't return to. The same papers which taunt and tempt her from their imprisoned state within those same boxes where they'd lain dormant in until their discovery. She cannot help but wonder now if it's the way they'd been meant to stay, if the words from the madwoman were never to have seen the light of day. How they were to be left forgotten to the turns of the world in its continuously unfolding history.

But the words sting and buzz within her mind unwilling to leave her alone or to give her peace for even a moment. No respite for her from the turn of words and phrases both frightening and sickening, exciting and enticing combined. They're marked with a complete absence or offering of any apology or excuse. They do not seek any either. They litter the pages in their angry scrawl without reason or explanation simply begging for an adherence to a plaintive call.

Sleep finally comes for her late in the night near its darkest edge, right before the trickle which hints at the sun's return and the start of a new day. In the first signs of deep and welcoming sleep, the Haunt is waiting for her with a horrible and crooked grin upon her face. The Haunt as the northern woman now refers to the madwoman, walks at will throughout her dreams and has since she'd made her presence known to her. The Haunt stalks the night inside her dreams once more turning them to her own purposes of nightmare. The Haunt has a twisty little smile on her face in pre-anticipatory joy at what she has planned for this evening's festivities. Her seemingly random killings are not as random as previously assumed or thought. For at least this evening they don't fit the pattern.

Images flicker faintly behind the northern woman's eyes. Eyes which are closed tighter than strictly necessary. An effort of her will to keep them closed against the fear that if she should open them she'd see how the images are not confined to her head. Her fear is the images are not fictions but her reality, and she's not only standing in the nightmare, but has become it.

The northern woman twists in her sleep trying hard to wake and failing. She thinks instead to stop the Haunt from its round of dastardly deeds and planned mayhem afoot tonight. The Haunt moves through areas familiar and not quite so though the northern woman thinks she recognizes the part of the city which the Haunt prowls tonight. Somewhere deep down she knows she's seen this very particular part of the city before with a familiarity which is frightening to her. It has some connection to her though she cannot fathom or tease out the what or why of this knowledge.

The Haunt even seems to turn to her and smile right at her. A sharp shark's mouth of teeth and a long lizard like tongue, which the northern woman is convinced is a distortion of the nightmare state. The Haunt nods her head for the northern woman to look forward as she spots tonight's meal and her pace is picking until she is a blur of black in speeded movement.

Blood flies, penetrates and soaks and some catches in her eyes, her ears, her nose, her mouth and her throat. It is a delicious, coppery warm taste and the smell of fresh warm blood fills the air as the very life is escaping from the man turned meal.

The poor bastard doesn't know what hit him, or shouldn't until she stops to tell him, to inform him of his imminent demise. She holds him up by his tattered shirt, his knees buckled and his toes scraping the ground. It's clear he's not capable of holding himself up and it's strictly by her will alone which allows him to even reach this semblance as his head lolls in an odd arc on his neck, broken from her over exuberance and inexperience with this newly found and terrible strength. His throat's gurgling as his blood's passing through the raggedly torn hole in his neck and chest right above his heart.

Her strength is as exhilarating as it is surprising. Strength a normal human woman shouldn't have. It's hers to command and to wield and such an excellent attribute to have, to feel its vibrancy like a hum of the tuning fork. Pardon, that's incorrect, it's more like the growl of a well-timed, well maintained engine at the peak of its performance with abilities waiting for the command to unleash all of its potency. This turns quickly into a cannot wait to demonstrate it desire, lending here a cocky edge with the feel of the power of being indestructible. She is untouchable, safe and free from harm.

There are no sharp teeth when the kill is made after a round of torture or taunt depending on which side of the argument you're standing on. There's but a kiss as the Haunt takes the soon to be departed by the throat, pulling the whimpering form close to her as she plants her lips on his. She breathes in deeply pulling the entirety of his essence within her. Hell, the northern woman almost expects some glow or light to transfer between the two, like in some cheap sci-fi serial, but there is none. The Haunt finishes and the body is allowed to drop with a thump to the ground like the empty vessel it now is.

The Haunt stands sated for the moment in delicious wicked pleasure of her action. Blood is in her mouth and covers her body, soaking her clothes and decorating her hands. She wants to jam one hand down into her pants in a masturbatory celebration as she's so turned on from the stalk and the kill, of the life taken and the incomparable, indescribable high of it.

The northern woman wakes up on her pallet her feet up on the balls with her back arching and her ass up off the floor. She's embarrassed to find her hands inside her panties, her fingers going at her clit like she's trying to get a confession. She's unable to stop herself and doesn't want to either despite the horrific connection of the killing dream and her current frenzied state of erotic arousal. This thought isn't helped when she experiences one of the most powerful orgasms of her life leaving her drained on her pallet and in a struggle to contemplate the meanings the dream world has presented in the course of the night's arc across the sky.

Guilt is the word for it, or should be, for the dream which had helped her give herself the number one most satisfying orgasm of her life, never to be topped. Murder even by proxy should not feel so good. Something so taboo in nearly every single human society on the planet and adding to the guilt in her pleasure though she knows she has the phrase just right. She finally understands the expression of *such guilty pleasure*. Yes and YES, and hell yes please! She finds she has her own little weird crooked grin upon her face. A new grin for her and one which she's not ever had prior to her brush against the previously fictional Haunt who was feeling more and more real with each passing night's scare.

Guilt put aside the northern woman stretches content on her pallet damn near purring. Sated in the moment or is until she takes a closer look at something she saw on her hands as they'd passed causally through her frame of vision in their return from their stretch overhead and back to her side. She takes a closer look at them and is horrified to find them covered in blood, the same hands which had just been in her panties and *inside her*.

The horror expands as she looks downward to see the blood staining her panties and lying congealed in a conspiratorial fashion within her most private parts, to her thighs and even down into the crack of her ass like a violation. She bolts for the shower tripping over her discarded shoes and jeans lying along the floor in her hurry for the blast of welcoming water. She looks down for a mere second in her passing but long enough for her to notice how they're also crusted with blood. She sees more when she arrives at the tub to discover it solidly ringed with the same stain as is the towel crumpled on the floor and the other one slung haphazardly over the bar above the tub from some previous activity which she cannot recall.

A scream rises up in a ripping fashion from her throat in a serious freak out. A straight solid what the fuck moment she wants desperately to get the hell away from, which she wants to cast it solidly backwards into the murky dark. She wants to cast doubt like a sorceress can against the all too real reality, and the ample evidence of blood she finds almost everywhere on and about her. God, so much blood everywhere. She receives one brief, clear moment of sanity or something as she checks herself for any cuts of her own or even if she has her period as some last ditch hope at explanation any amount of the blood. She logically knows there is no way short of bled to death which could possibly account for all of this blood. It's a grasp on her part, a desperation for explanation of any sort other than the clear one offered up to her. It's a wish and a prayer for this to be anything other than it is. Dear God in heaven, hear her prayer. Are you listening? Are you there? Because she could really use some help right now. She silently wonders at the same time if it's a sacrilege to only call on a god, to only offer up prayers to a being you're half certain isn't there anyway and only when you need something desperately from that same said being.

She comes to the conclusion with a sudden and violent clarity. She no longer has to wonder about going fucking insane or dreaming one way or the other as it is these types of definitions which no longer matter now. She's lost deep within the living nightmare which she has no hope of ever escaping from. The sad conclusion reached if she's neither dreaming nor insane and there's no use in her denying this new reality of hers any longer. There is too much gore and blood covering her, in which her feet slip where she stands. Which is everywhere upon her and place she can see. It is caked upon her in spots and glopped deep into her hair and stuck to her scalp, and, oh god. Even in her mouth and down her throat. Caked between her teeth and lying along her tongue providing ample proof to the realness of things for her now.

She stares at her betraying hands with wide eyed revulsion, disgusted with the horror they've wrought and still covered, she realizes, with blood and sinew as plain proof of what she'd done. She holds her hands away from her as if she can distance herself from them when she hears a laugh. The laugh she'd like to describe as evil taunting her. Its mocking in its tone when she falls down on her knees and vomits into the carnage about her feet.

The nightmare of the Haunt invading her is still too vivid, too fresh. The Haunt taking her in her sleep and then out on the town and her travels but most especially with her to her kills. The mayhem brings a shudder of revulsion creepy crawling under the northern woman's skin as opposed to along or atop it and is seriously freaking her the fuck out. She wants to claw at her own skin, to rend her own flesh from off her own bones, to rip into the flesh and dig out the offending,

illegal presence crawling therein and to remove it from her
person.

She wants to scream once more when she takes in the
scene of her small space. She's dismayed at the horror she
finds all about her including the mass of the mess she stands
in. It's a soon to be critical and vomitus mistake as she
recognizes faces, or at least parts of faces in the gore. They're
the same faces she'd seen in the nightmare, faces of those
who'd been murdered at the hands of the Haunt.

The northern woman attempts to order her brain, to
apply her intellect to the problem. College should be good for
something but she cannot form thoughts. She cannot rally
herself to any move or action, to do something. She's unable to
draw any solid conclusions to what all of this might mean, let
alone being able to answer in some small form just what in the
fuck is happening to her. The Haunt has committed one of her
usual mayhems while simultaneously finding a way to
incriminate the northern woman.

The Haunt had seized possession of her body to
commit her mayhem. She has left the northern woman covered
in blood and ankle deep in the carnage as evidence of the
deeds done. She only has a faint flickering dreamlike memory

of the event in her mind. This, deliberate pause, is the sole *reasonable* explanation for what has transpired as opposed to a descent into outright fucking insanity. It's a comforting thought as it allows the northern woman to insistently cling to her claim of innocence. To her continued refusal to acknowledge the blood on her own hands and body even as she washes it away.

Later she'll burn her clothes and boots knowing how these are not the acts of an innocent person despite her protestations of innocence otherwise. She *is* innocent though, and these actions will ensure it leaving one story to be told about the night prior's activities. She adds insurance to the proclamations as she continues to work hiding the madwoman's crimes, catching herself continuously blurring the line uncomfortably. She has to keep reminding herself she's not the perpetrator. How it's the work of the other, the Haunt of a woman who no one's seen in five years or more. The Haunt is the responsible party even if the northern woman cannot explain or prove it otherwise. It's a taunt of hope which she clings to frantically as slim as it is and smacking as a large quantity of desperation. It's all she presently has as she tries to calm herself in order to then tackle the quandary facing her.

But one disaster at a time.

As she works to cleanse herself and the space about her, she returns for a moment to her earlier wonder at the possibility of insanity. She's almost longing for the period prior, when it had still held an offering of lightness to her predicament. Pining for the moment when insanity as an answer feels almost welcome now as compared to her present circumstances which are all too clearly and starkly drawn.

She swears she hears a wicked laugh again which is at once recognizable and yet alien to her. It elicits her own brittle cracked laugh as she huddles on her knees in a prayer-like pose without any plan or will to do any actual praying. It's fine really. She wouldn't know whom to direct any prayer towards anyway other than to her madwoman tormentor.

The idea of a prayer to the Haunt strikes her at once as too funny in a strongly ironic sense before she considers the possibility. It's as real as any other might or could possibly be and might work as well as any other fictitious. She perhaps wrongly feels there wasn't anything more she could possibly lose and felt deliriously free from all such dangers and beyond such omens out in the great wide open.

Down the Rabbit Hole

Late October appropriately arrives when she accepts the nightmare as her new reality, no longer stuck in deniability. It's one of the stages of grieving if she recalls as she moves down the list. She knows without any trace or hint of doubt anymore how it was she and not the Haunt who'd committed the murder. Or is it multiple murders now which she's scarily blended into one singular act. Sadly, the previous question is almost of no matter for its inability, its incapability, of easing the burden of carrying those deeds around. They cannot offer her forgiveness for placing them, however mistakenly, as the dream actions of the woman which she'd been referring to as the Haunt.

She's stopped with the name, any name really to refer to her by anymore as too dangerous to say anymore in any fashion. The northern woman is silently horrified at the deeds done. The act committed had not been as hard a task to complete as she would've hoped it would be. As she would've previously never thought herself capable of, let alone a skill she'd possessed. She now hears more clearly the Haunt's mocking, haunting laughter despite its distance from her, a distances measured in more than miles. The mocking laugh arrives as it's supposed to, as a taunt with a side of melancholy music to ride in on to the present place and time.

Murders done and ugly information gained information which no one should rightly know and which is kept away from the general public for good reason. Good reason she only knows in the aftermath of the murder: no one goes quietly or well. First-hand knowledge hard won and measured against a cost of what, which the northern woman didn't rightly know though she strongly suspected, was any sense of decency she'd had within her, any good taken from her along with her soul. It was seemingly as the Haunt had lain out for her when she'd first not heeded any warnings given. Her personal price to pay and now the bill come due.

The northern woman knows there's no cure for whatever this is. This state of being she has found herself stepped over into now. It's not quite living and sure as shit ain't quite dead either. It is rather something else entirely, something in-between and indistinct. There's no holy man or woman who can lead her from the proverbial darkness to the proverbial light. No ghost whisperer to help her gain closure with the things which are now lost. It's all gone, despite an occasionally glimpse which can be seen at the edges of her vision past the reach of outstretched fingertips. Such futility, such exercises in pointlessness these thoughts, when, what remains are things which are broken and soon, too soon perhaps, these broken things become obscure and then forgotten. Lost forever in a sea of all kinds of things and no longer surprised for the dislocation.

Deep sorrow takes up permanent residence deep within her. Sorrow at the deaths and for the haunting woman who'd stalked her dreams and still might. Sorrow for the city by the hands of a storm, for the person in her dream and at her feet killed by her own hands, and lastly, for her own death. The death of the person she used to be but who, she's certain, is to be no more. You cannot walk through whatever kind of an event this presently was and come out the other side the same. Things cannot be unseen and more importantly they cannot be undone.

Time for her to face things now, to own up to it, to no longer place blame at the feet of the Haunt, time for her to admit to herself how it had been her all along. The northern woman is faced with too much incontrovertible evidence to blame anyone else for anything which had been wrought. It was no longer any matter the scattered scribblings of a madwoman tossed back into the far corners of a house now lost from the face of the earth. The madwoman's papers lost and forgotten misplaced once more to remain uncared for, as perhaps they'd always meant to be left as. And the Haunt herself has gone into the night to where the northern woman knows not.

The northern woman swears she can clearly hear the Haunt still laughing somewhere far off across the city despite her absence otherwise. The laugh being faintly carried along on the wind on a metallic tone and right to her, loudly and clearly and right to her for her to know it, recognize it and feel it.

The Haunt is most pleased with herself about the lesson taught combined with a strong sense of satisfaction at the work she'd done.

So, maybe now the Haunt can get some of the much desired rest she'd contemplated seemingly another lifetime ago. If rest is not to be had though, if it's unavailable to her and her kind; then perhaps she can acquire a mocking equivalent by simply sitting still and letting the world spin round her for a moment or more til she decides to step back aboard.

This thought pleases her in perversely unknowable ways bringing her crooked smile back to her face. She contemplates sharing the thought with The Man of The Waters as she thought he alone with his distinct perspective could really appreciate the humor there. She even takes a step in his direction but thinks better of it and steps instead in the opposite direction and away from the river for now. She steps towards the Quarter and Molly's for a pint or more to avoid thinking for a little while, time for her to take some of it for herself before she goes and decides anything further.

Thin lines reprise themselves. They've been crossed despite the warning sign posted though it offered little to hint at the dangers. This is the current truth and lie she tells herself. It is her favorite form of denial, as she seeks to separate herself from her part, to accept her own role in the events as they've unfolded. If she could work past her own anger at the betrayal she lays at the doorstep of the universes, she might be able to see it. To see how there were indeed plenty of warnings given, placed, issued or anyway other which you may care to describe them. They were there for her to recognize if she'd but paused for one moment to pay them their due. She'd been in too big an all-fired hurry to heed even the blatantly placed signs and was now lost on the other side of those thin lines unknowingly crossed. She is without guide or guidance in this new territory unless you included the fading and moving away from her wicked laugh of the madwoman Haunt. And she did not.

Transference

She is now what she once feared she'd become, was becoming. What once was too intimidating to contemplate is now her current condition. A situation beyond remedy and a fair shot past redemption in this altered state of grace.

She's now not so interested in those concepts or things any longer. They don't mean the same things or share the same values over here in the in-between or wherever this is where she's found herself. There is an entirely different form of language over here on this side of the thin line. One which simply doesn't translate, not directly anyway when there are so many options. So many different kinds of meanings and all of them without application or meaning or sense here. They fall to the floor, briefly stirring the dust which they secretly long to turn back to because they're so tired of carrying the weight of all of their very heavy definitions.

Impossible words made meaningless in their definition or judgment even if they decide against her. They cannot compete though when weighed versus the joy, oh the sheer joy of it all. The absolutely pure joy of life, if a little poetic license is allowed, beyond the natural rule of law she's no longer beholden to. She rejoices in the blessedness granted her in the hunt under the night's ever loving embrace of the eternal night, her empire and lover, and willing to hold her for as long as the moon will continue to rise.

Once she was, and now she is. Though she doesn't know what this may be. She doesn't know the why to this state of being or if there even is a why. She's uncertain if she wants any more certainty. She wonders if there's any comfort to be found in the why of this, but is more worried about if there is *not* any comfort here. Besides, knowing things as she knows them now, she's placing a heavy bet on there not being a reason to it or a why for it. All she really needs to know anyway is the here and now on the other side of the surprisingly thin line.

The cross over to this in-between life is more like what Morrison sang about in the great Doors song of long ago, like he'd known what she'd only just learned. A 'slip on through' minus any drama involved or just the irony of this one lone song dancing round her head at the moment. Luckily it's most appropriate for the scene. She appreciates the tunage on her journey. There's nothing like a good jam to cure some road woes and she smirks at the joy of the idea. Pardon, more like a sneer, and one she stole from Billy Idol and plans on wearing out - soon and often.

There's a smile rising up on her lips slightly ahead of the war cry ready to find voice as her head rises. It's a crooked, wicked smile in match of one formerly described and a reflection of her current state of mind. She can feel the night calling to her and an excitement rising up in her body. It's rising up to be released as an unearthly war cry rising from her as a challenge to the night past her sweet lips to lay claim to her part of the night. She reserving a piece for her in a most proprietary manner. A delicious and wicked little mirthful laugh follows out after the cry though not as far reaching. She wants to shout out a curse to the Haunt for leading her here, but knows it was her and her alone responsible for the fall.

A hunger wakes deep within her, a hunger almost insatiable and all compelling. The hunger as a side element just as strong and compelling, an urge to mayhem, a want to destruction which she knows to feed once is to feed it forever. The hunger an insatiable want which will always demand and always crave more than can possibly be given with it in its ever increasing demands of her.

Well, there's at least one positive result to this present condition, the freedom granted from fear. And why should she fear when death holds sway no longer and natural laws seem to no longer apply. Death the Eternal may be a little pissed about this blasphemy against her reign, this blight and insult to the natural order of things standing as two Haunts do outside what most would describe as the natural order of things. Death, the undefeated champion, forced into an unnatural period of waiting on them and both content to leave her waiting a little longer; things to do after all.

The former northern woman has accepted the mantle pressed upon her in her nightmares by the madwoman Haunt and now she is sworn to be the nightmare to others.

She's intoxicated on the premise writ and ripped from the pages penned by the Haunt as she bursts outside and into a light rain. She dares once more to shout a name out at the night sky to all of the frights prowling the dark.

First, a name given.

Second, a rest disturbed.

Third, a name called and left carelessly on the wind.

Warnings unheeded, dangers unmindfully ignored.

Peril now, the destination of choice.

Mind the darkness now.

It's the place she calls home.

And never, ever, dare call her name or anything else at all.

Lest you want an answer from her after all.

ABOUT THE AUTHOR

Jack Kelly is a pseudonym.

WAKE THE DEAD is his second book.

See Her Start
in

Also available through Amazon.com

And On Kindle